Collect the special coins in this book.
You will earn one gold coin for
every chapter you read.

Once you have finished all the chapters,
find out what to do with your gold coins at
the back of the book.

www.beastquest.co.uk

ORCHARD BOOKS
Carmelite House
50 Victoria Embankment
London EC4Y 0DZ

A Paperback Original
First published in Great Britain in 2008
This edition published in 2015

A CIP catalogue record for this book is available from
the British Library.

ISBN 978 1 40834 771 3

1

Printed and bound by CPI Group (UK) Ltd, Croydon, CR0 4YY

Orchard Books
An imprint of Hachette Children's Group
Part of The Watts Publishing Group Limited
An Hachette UK Company

www.hachette.co.uk

Beast Quest®

Soltra
The Stone Charmer

BY ADAM BLADE

ORCHARD

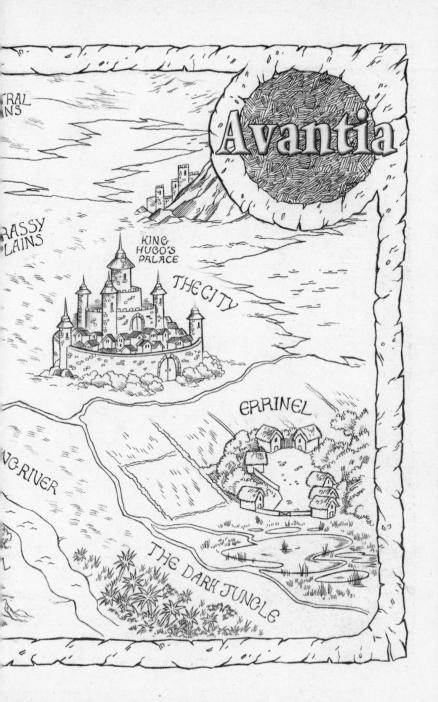

CONTENTS

Did you think it was over?

Did you think I would accept defeat, and disappear?

No! That can never be. I am Malvel, the Dark Wizard who strikes fear into the hearts of the people of Avantia. I still have much more to show this kingdom, and one boy in particular...Tom.

The young hero liberated the six Beasts of Avantia from my curse. But his fight is far from over. Let us see how he fares with a new Quest, one that will surely crush him and his companion, Elenna.

Avantia's Beasts had good hearts that I corrupted for my own wicked purpose. Now, thanks to Tom, they are free to protect the kingdom once more. But now I bring to Avantia six Beasts whose hearts are evil and so cannot be set free: monster squid, giant monkey, stone charmer, snake man, king of spiders and three-headed lion. Each one guards a piece of the most precious relic of Avantia, which I have stolen: the suit of Golden Armour that gives magical strengths to its rightful owner. I will stop at nothing to prevent Tom collecting the complete suit and defeating me again. This time he will not win!

Malvel

PROLOGUE

It had been a long day for the farmer. He plodded along the earth furrows behind his two oxen. Sweat dripped down his neck as he guided the heavy plough through the soil.

The sun was setting over the marsh that lay to the west of the farm. The farmer looked up, then frowned, lifting an arm to mop his brow. Dense fog was beginning to creep from the marsh across the field. It was unusual for it to be so thick at this time of year.

Shivering a little, he unharnessed the oxen and began to lead them towards the stable. The animals were usually eager for their meal at day's end, but now the farmer could hardly get them to move. He snapped the leather harness, then frowned. It had become icy cold in his fingers. He turned. The two oxen had come to a dead halt.

"What's wrong, lads?" he asked, walking back to the animals. Tendrils of fog encircled them all, cutting them off from the farmhouse. He patted the neck of one ox, then let out a shocked gasp. Instead of warm flesh, his hand had struck a hard, cold surface.

The two animals had turned to stone!

As he looked into the oxen's great brown eyes – which were still moving, wide and rolling with fear – he saw a shadowy, milky outline reflected in them. Something or someone was standing right behind him.

He turned, crying out in terror as he stared at the female figure that had stepped from the heart of the fog. The setting sun glowed behind her.

The woman was two heads

taller than him, her body swathed
in a shining, rippling garment –
like a cloak made of black water.
He gazed up into the woman's face
– but found that she *had* no face,

just a featureless surface, marble smooth and milky white.

Then the final terror came.

The whole of her face folded up on itself like a huge eyelid – and from beneath that eyelid stared a single great eye, its stare unblinking.

The farmer stared into the unblinking eye and suddenly his fear slipped away.

"Beautiful," he murmured. "It's... so...beautiful..."

He took a step towards her.

She lifted an arm and held out a white hand towards him. He grasped it, close enough now to see his own reflection in the great eye. Crystals of ice filled his veins, deadening his limbs, freezing his heart.

Moments later, like his oxen, only the farmer's eyes could move. His body was encased in stone.

The woman turned, her silhouette undulating as she drifted back into the fog.

A few moments later, the farmer saw a movement out of the corner of his eye. A small boy was crouching in terror behind the low dry-stone wall that marked the boundary of the field. He tried to call to the boy, to ask him to fetch help, but the only sound that escaped him was a groan.

Terrified, the boy ran towards the village.

The fog curled around the farmer's shoulders like a shroud. How long would it be before death took him?

HOMEWARD BOUND

"At last!" gasped Tom as he pushed past a branch and found himself gazing out over open countryside.

"Thank goodness!" said Elenna from behind him. "I was beginning to think the Dark Jungle went on for ever."

They stepped out into the cool of the late afternoon, exhausted and glad to be free of the dark, sultry heat.

Ahead of them, the land sloped downwards in grassy terraces to a wide, winding river that rushed through deep stony banks. Tom took one final glance back into the sinister jungle, thinking about his battle with Claw the Giant Monkey, and remembering how he had just managed to snatch the golden chainmail from the Beast.

Silver, Elenna's faithful wolf, and Storm, Tom's noble stallion, emerged from the jungle, too. Silver bounded and barked joyfully, and Storm neighed and pranced.

"They're glad to be out in the open," Elenna said. "Can we camp for the night down by the river? I could catch us some fish for our supper."

Tom looked thoughtfully at her and sighed.

"What's wrong?" she asked.

"I was thinking about Aduro," he replied. "I'm worried about what Malvel might have done to him."

The Dark Wizard had kidnapped their friend and protector, Aduro – Avantia's Good Wizard. Malvel had appeared to them in a vision after Tom's defeat of Claw, showing them torn strips of Aduro's blue cloak.

Is he even still alive? Tom wondered.

But whatever fate had befallen Aduro, Tom knew that he still had to fulfil his Quest and unite the six parts of the Golden Armour that Malvel had stolen and scattered across the kingdom. Aduro had told them it was the only way they could rescue him. Unless they succeeded, Avantia would never be safe from the six Evil Beasts set loose by Malvel.

The friends and their two animal companions made their way to the river. A valley brought them down to a shingled beach.

Tom watched as Elenna waded into the water with an arrow fixed to her bow. After a long wait, she shot the arrow, and a moment later was splashing her way up to the shore with a large salmon. She left it on a rock and went back to catch some more.

Silver sniffed the fish but shook his big shaggy head and trotted off. Tom guessed that he was on the prowl for something he'd find a bit tastier. Storm was grazing contentedly on some long grass.

Tom felt tired and homesick as he looked at the racing river, thinking how different it was from the wide, still lake beside his home village of Errinel. He had not seen it for a long time now.

He shook himself and started to gather wood. Then he lit a fire. He made two tripods of sturdy twigs and skewered the salmon on another twig to hang it above the flames. Soon Elenna came back with two more fish.

The twilight deepened as the fish cooked, and, as they ate, Tom told Elenna about his home. "The lake is as clear as crystal," he said. "On hot summer evenings everyone goes to the lake's shore to eat, play music and watch the sunset."

"It sounds lovely," Elenna said through a mouthful of salmon.

"People say that the water has healing properties," Tom continued, gazing at the darkening sky. "The water has to be collected as the sun sets." He laughed. "It's just a legend," he said. "I don't suppose it's true."

"It's a nice story, all the same," Elenna said. "And after all that we've seen, who knows what's true and what isn't? Most people think the Beasts are a myth, but we know they're not."

After they had finished their meal, Tom and Elenna went to check on their companions. Silver was lying with his head between his paws, snoring softly. Storm stood close by, dozing peacefully.

The two friends found a place to spread their bedrolls for the night. The pieces of armour that Tom had already recovered were by his side. The golden helmet, forged into the shape of an eagle's head, gleamed softly in the glowing starlight.
He reached out and touched the chainmail vest, wondering about the Master of the Beasts who had worn

it before him. Then he thought of his own father, Taladon the Swift, who had undertaken a Beast Quest of his own years ago, but had disappeared. *I wish I had known him*, he thought drowsily. He hoped that one day they might be reunited.

The next day dawned bright and warm, the sun rising in a clear blue sky. Tom unrolled the magical map of Avantia that Aduro had given him when his adventures first began.

As he studied it, the map came to life. Meadow grasses moved in the wind and the tiny mountains were cold to the touch. The forests and rivers, villages and castles were

all miniature versions of the real landscape of Avantia.

A glowing red path usually appeared on the map, showing Tom where to find his next challenge, but so far there was no sign of it.

"There!" exclaimed Elenna after they had been staring at the map for a little while.

A tiny point of golden light was glowing on the map. As Tom and Elenna peered, it pulsed and grew larger until they could make out the shape of a golden breastplate.

"It's the next piece of armour!" Elenna said.

Tom let out a cry of delight. "Yes!" he gasped. "And look where it is!" He pointed to a wide, clear lake set in rich farmlands. Beside the lake nestled a small village. "It's Errinel, my home! You'll be able to meet Uncle Henry and Aunt Maria who brought me up." Tom felt his eyes fill with tears. "I haven't seen them since I started the Quests," he said.

A large muzzle snuffled close to his

ear. It was Silver, his eyes bright with understanding. Tom turned with a grin. Storm was close by, pawing at the shingle with a hoof.

"You can't hide your feelings from us!" Elenna said with a laugh. "We know how much you want to go home! Come on – let's pack up camp and get going."

"Yes!" Tom laughed. "And no stopping till we get to Errinel!"

But his laughter soon faded as he thought of his Quest and the dangers that lay ahead. He had to get to Errinel quickly – but what kind of Beast would be waiting there for them?

And what harm had it already done to his home and his family?

TURNED TO STONE

Tom and Elenna sat astride Storm's
broad back as he cantered along,
with Silver loping at his side.
Despite the perils that lay ahead,
Tom was glad to be heading home.
The journey to Erinnel had been easy
so far, following the weaving line
of the river. The day was hot, but a
fresh breeze kept them cool. Brightly

coloured butterflies and jewelled dragonflies danced over the water.

"We're nearly there," Tom said at last. A thrill of excitement shot through him at the thought of seeing his uncle and aunt again. But this would be no ordinary homecoming. The image of a golden breastplate had brought him here, and that could only mean one of Malvel's Beasts was lurking near the village.

"We should leave the river now and go up over that low hill," Tom said, pointing. "There's a small wood on the other side, and then it's all farmland till we get to Errinel."

"I'm really looking forward to seeing where you grew up," Elenna said.

They rode up the gentle slope of the hill and down into the woods. Silver trotted beside them, sniffing the air as if he were trying to pick up a scent.

"What is it, boy?" Elenna asked. "Can you smell something?"

The wolf let out a soft whine. Storm whickered and turned his head. Something was unsettling the animals. Tom's hand went to his sword hilt. His shield, which carried six magical tokens from the Good Beasts of Avantia, was slung over his shoulder. He had freed all the Beasts from Malvel's evil curse – Ferno the Fire Dragon, Sepron the Sea Serpent, Arcta the Mountain Giant, Tagus the Horse-Man, Nanook the Snow Monster and Epos the Flame Bird – and he knew he could call on them if he was in trouble. In addition, the golden chainmail and helmet he had already retrieved from Zepha the Monster Squid and Claw the Giant Monkey were close at hand in the saddlebag. The chainmail gave him strength of heart and the helmet sharpened his sight. His powers were growing with every Quest. He was ready for battle.

"I think there's danger nearby," he murmured.

Elenna nodded, sliding an arrow from the quiver and slotting it into her bowstring.

Slowly they came out of the woods and made their way along a road between high hedges. Through gaps in the hedgerows, they could see fields all around them, and the occasional distant farmhouse or barn.

"It all seems normal enough," Tom said warily. "Except…" He frowned. There was something wrong, but he couldn't put his finger on it. And then it struck him. "It's too quiet. What's happened to all the birds?"

"There's a row of starlings over there," Elenna said, pointing to a wooden gate ahead of them in the hedgerow.

Tom peered at the birds as they approached. He expected them to take fright and flap away over the fields. But they didn't move. The hair prickled on the back of his neck.

Tom slid down from the saddle and walked up to the birds, then let out a breath as he realised they were just statues. He reached out to touch one of them. The bird's body was hard and cold.

"They aren't real," he called back. "They're made of stone."

Elenna jumped down and ran over

to his side. She touched one of the small statues, then leaned in closer. "You can see every tiny detail of the feathers," she said. "They're too perfect to have been carved. Tom, I don't like this."

Then Tom spotted something in the field beyond – a grey-brown shape in the stubble of newly cropped hay.

He climbed the gate and walked over to the shape, crouching down beside it and reaching out a hand. It was a stone hare, its long limbs stretched as if it had been frozen in mid-flight. Tom picked it up and carried it back to the gate. He laid it at the roadside and stared down at it with a frown.

Silver moved hesitantly towards

the hare and sniffed it. A moment later, he bounded away, snorting and shaking his muzzle.

Elenna shivered. "What are you thinking?" she asked Tom.

He looked at her. "I don't believe they're statues at all," he said. "I think something has turned living creatures into stone."

"It must be the Evil Beast," Elenna murmured.

A new urgency filled Tom's heart. "We have to get to the village," he said. "Let's hope the Beast hasn't been there yet." The thought of his aunt and uncle and the other villagers of Errinel turned to stone was too awful.

The two friends jumped back

into Storm's saddle.

Tom pressed his heels into the stallion's sides and the horse broke into a gallop. Silver ran close by, his body low to the ground.

The village was a few miles away through the fields. Tom remembered the fragment of horseshoe given to him by Tagus the Horse-Man. It had the power to give him great speed.

He touched the magical token in his shield and Storm began to gallop faster than Tom had ever known. He clung on to Storm's back as the stallion flew through the fields, and Elenna gripped Tom's belt as the wind whistled past their ears. Silver bounded alongside the racing horse, his tongue lolling.

Only a few moments later Tom saw something strange ahead of them in a nearby field.

"Stop!" he called.

Storm came to a halt. Tom jumped down and ran towards a low fence.

"I know this field," he called to Elenna as she leapt off the stallion's back. "It belongs to Farmer Gretlin.

Look!" He pointed a shaking finger over the fence.

Three grey figures stood unmoving in the newly ploughed field: a team of oxen and a man. All had been turned to stone.

3

A SWORD TO THE HEART

Tom stood on the bottom bar of the fence and stared out across the desolate field.

"The Beast could still be nearby," he said worriedly. "And it could turn us into stone!" He strode back towards Storm. "I have to be prepared for anything."

He slipped on the heavy

chainmail and pulled on the golden helmet. Now he would feel no fear and be able to see the Beast if it was still lurking. He climbed back

into the saddle, slipping his shield over his left arm and loosening his sword in its scabbard.

Elenna scrambled up behind him, her bow ready on her shoulder, her quiver of arrows to hand.

"Go, boy!" Tom said to Storm, nudging with his heels. The stallion backed away from the fence, then, with a surge of power, he leapt forward and took the fence in one long, smooth jump.

Fearlessly, Storm cantered towards the frozen stone figures, the ever-loyal Silver by his side.

Tom could feel Elenna's fingers slipping on the polished chainmail as they rode, but he had no fear of her falling – she was too good a rider for that. He expected an attack from the Beast, but they crossed the field without harm. The two animals were uneasy, however, as if they sensed that danger was close at hand.

Everything was eerily silent as they stopped by the stone figures. Tom and Elenna slid down from the saddle. Storm neighed nervously and backed away. Silver circled the man and his oxen, sniffing the air, his ears down and the fur along his back as stiff as wire.

"It's Farmer Gretlin!" Tom cried, as he and Elenna drew closer. Cautiously, he reached out and touched the stone man's chest. It was cold.

Elenna frowned. "He looks happy," she said, as she gazed into the farmer's face. "I don't understand. Why would someone who is about to be turned to stone be so happy?"

"Malvel's Beasts are usually terrifying," Tom said. He felt confused. "This must have been done by something that looks harmless, but isn't."

"Something beautiful, even," added Elenna.

"Beautiful and deadly," Tom said grimly. "This is bad, Elenna. How do you fight something that doesn't seem dangerous?"

"What do you think the Beast looks like?" asked Elenna.

Tom gazed sadly into the

farmer's face. "The only person who could tell us has been killed," he murmured. But then he looked more closely, staring up into the farmer's eyes. Was it his imagination or had he seen movement?

"Elenna," Tom said urgently. "I think he's alive."

His friend looked carefully. "You could be right," she said. As she moved nearer, her elbow struck the statue. It made a curiously hollow sound.

Tom rapped his knuckles against the statue's arm. Again, they heard the hollow noise.

"The stone is just a shell around him," Tom cried.

"But how can we break the shell without hurting him?" Elenna asked.

Tom drew his sword.

"You can't!" Elenna gasped. "You'll kill him."

"Not if I find the weak point," Tom said. "My uncle is a blacksmith, remember? He taught me always to search for the weak spot, and then to use it." He circled the farmer. "There has to be a crack or a fault line somewhere," he muttered. "There has to be!" Suddenly he noticed a hairline crack in the stone chest – just above the man's heart.

"There!" he said. He lifted his sword and carefully placed the lethal tip against the crack.

"No!" Elenna cried out. "It's too dangerous. If you slip – if you make one wrong move – the blade will go into his heart."

"I won't slip," Tom said. "And we have no choice. We can't leave him like this, and we need him to tell us what the Beast looks like."

"Be careful," Elenna whispered, stepping back as Tom readied himself for the blow. But he felt very sure of himself, and the golden helmet gave him perfect vision as he guided the point of his sword towards the crack.

He twisted the blade and pushed it into the stone.

Nothing happened. Frowning,

Tom drew back his hand and slammed his palm hard against the hilt of the sword. He heard Elenna give a gasp of alarm. Storm and Silver were watching with worried eyes.

He struck the hilt a second time. The stone rang but the crack held.

This was no time to give up. Tom hit the hilt a third time. He saw the crack widen. A web of fractures spun out across the farmer's chest and down his limbs.

Then the stone shell shattered
into fragments and tumbled to the
ground.

Farmer Gretlin's chest gave a
great heave as he sucked air into

his lungs and fell forward onto
his hands and knees, gasping and
coughing.

He was alive!

INTO THE WOODS

Tom took a water bottle from Storm's saddlebag and bent down to give it to the gasping farmer. As he drank, Elenna stood over him, an arrow at the ready, her keen eyes scanning the empty field.

"Who are you?" Farmer Gretlin asked, still breathing heavily.

Tom took off his helmet and grinned.

"Tom!" exclaimed the farmer.
"You've saved my life! Help me up."
He put a hand on Tom's shoulder and
got shakily to his feet.

"What did this to you?" Elenna
asked.

The farmer gave her a curious look.
"And who are *you*?"

"She's my friend, Elenna," Tom
said. "We're here to help. Can you tell
us what happened?"

The farmer's eyes narrowed. "There
was fog over the marsh," he said.
"And a tall lady dressed in black."
A shudder went through him. "She
had no face, just a huge eye. It was
the most beautiful thing I've ever
seen. And then I couldn't move."
He smiled gratefully at them. "Until

you came to my aid."

"How long ago was this?" Tom asked.

The farmer shook his head. "A day," he said uncertainly. "Maybe more."

"Who can this woman be?" Tom wondered aloud, as the farmer and Elenna went to check on the stone oxen.

His heart began to race as a familiar cruel voice whispered in his ear. "Would you like to meet Soltra the Stone Charmer face to face?"

"Malvel!" Tom spun round, but saw nothing. "I'm not afraid of you, or any of your Evil Beasts."

The Dark Wizard let out a laugh like the hissing of snakes. "There is no victory for you here, boy. Soltra cannot be beaten."

"I'll beat her!"Tom snarled. "Just you wait and see!"

But there was no reply – the voice was gone.

Tom gripped his sword, wishing he could put the cold steel into Malvel's wicked heart.

"The Beast is called Soltra," he said to Elenna, as she came back. He looked over to Farmer Gretlin, who was still standing by the stone oxen. "Malvel just spoke to me. He says she can't be beaten."

"I don't believe that," Elenna said. "We'll find a way!"

Tom nodded. "You're right. We should go to the village – and let's hope she hasn't been there before us." Had his uncle and aunt already fallen victim to Soltra? He tried not to think about it.

They walked over to the farmer, Storm and Silver following with wide, watchful eyes.

"Can you bring these creatures back to life?" Farmer Gretlin asked.

Tom stared carefully at the two animals. There wasn't the faintest sign of life in their stony eyes. He shook his head regretfully. "I'm sorry," he said.

Tom and Elenna helped the farmer across the ploughed field, Storm and Silver on either side, then walked along the winding road that led to the village. Tom gazed around, memories flooding back, as the familiar rooftops and chimneys of Errinel came into sight above the hedgerows and trees.

The village was silent and deserted, save for three grey statues: one woman carrying a woven basket; another laying out wares on a market stall; and a man with his arm lifted, as if he were trying to shield his eyes from the sun. Soltra had been here.

A lump filled Tom's throat. He remembered the village square as a place filled with noise and bustle as the cheerful people of Errinel went about their daily lives, not this empty, desolate silence. He examined the three statues but could not find a single crack to help him break their

stone prisons. Farmer Gretlin had
been lucky.

An urgent fear built inside Tom as
he ran from house to house, hoping
desperately to find someone who

had managed to survive Soltra's enchantment. But there was no one.

"The rest of the villagers must have fled," Farmer Gretlin said.

They came to the forge where Tom's Uncle Henry worked. The familiar bellows lay beside the fire, and the iron-working tools were set out on the worktable as usual.

"Where has everyone gone?" asked Farmer Gretlin. "How are we to find them?"

Tom gave a grim smile. "We have a wolf, don't we?" he said. He called to Silver, and the wolf padded into the forge and looked questioningly up at him. Tom took an old leather apron down from a peg on the wall. "Here, Silver," he said. "This will have Uncle Henry's scent."

Silver sniffed at the apron. A moment later, he let out a sharp bark and ran from the forge.

"Follow him!" Tom cried. "He's got the scent!"

Silver glided along, his body low, his muzzle to the ground, moving fast but stopping every now and then to allow the others to catch up. Soon he was leading them towards dense woodland on the other side of the town.

Tom turned to Farmer Gretlin. "Will you stay in the village in case anyone comes back?" he asked. "And keep Storm with you?"

"I will," said the farmer. "Good luck."

Leaving Storm and the farmer, Tom and Elenna followed Silver. They pushed their way through brambles and ferns, only just keeping the speeding wolf in sight as they plunged deeper and deeper into the woods.

Soon they came to a dell filled with a tangle of ivy and briars. There was no sign of Silver.

A few moments later, a sharp bark broke the silence. Tom turned and ran towards the sound, but he had only gone a few steps when his foot caught in a snarl of ivy roots. He sprawled headlong.

"Tom! Are you all right?" called a familiar voice.

Tom struggled to his feet as Aunt

Maria emerged from the cover of the trees, her face filled with joy and concern. And right behind her was Uncle Henry.

They were safe!

5

REUNION

Tom was caught up in a huge bear hug by his aunt and uncle, and for a few moments he forgot all about the danger they faced.

"How many of you escaped?" he asked.

Villagers stepped out of cover and stood uneasily around him, their faces pale and anxious.

"We're all safe," said Uncle Henry.

"All those who ran." He frowned at Tom. "But how did you know what had happened?"

Tom looked thoughtfully at his uncle and aunt and the gathered villagers. Aduro had always told him not to talk to the ordinary folk of Avantia about the Beasts, but people from Errinel had been turned to stone by Soltra – and the others deserved to know what she was.

He raised his voice so that everyone would be able to hear him. "What I'm going to tell you is the deepest secret in all Avantia, and no one must ever speak of it outside the village," he told them. "I am under the guidance of Wizard

Aduro, adviser to King Hugo. I have come here with my friends, Elenna, Storm and Silver, to kill the stone charmer, an Evil Beast."

There was a murmur of amazement. Uncle Henry stepped forward. "You are the true son of your father," he said solemnly. "And I see from your face, and from the weapons and armour you bear, that you are ready for your challenge." He smiled grimly. "Tell us what we should do."

It made Tom feel proud that Uncle Henry knew he could be trusted with such an important task.

"Soltra seems to have left the village for now," he said. "We should go back there for rest and food. If I am to defeat her, I need to know everything that happened in Errinel."

When they returned to the blacksmith's house, Aunt Maria warmed up a stew she had made, while Uncle Henry told Tom and Elenna how a village boy had seen Soltra with Farmer Gretlin at sunset, and had run to warn the others.

"That is how most of us managed to escape before the Beast came," Aunt Maria said, as she ladled the hearty stew into wooden bowls for Tom and Elenna.

"So Soltra appeared at sunset last night," Tom said. "That could mean she can't survive in full daylight. It would be her one weakness."

"It's already late afternoon," Elenna pointed out. "The sun will be setting soon."

"I know," Tom said. "We don't have much time." He looked at his uncle. "We should lead the villagers to the shores of the lake for safety."

"The lake?" Uncle Henry said in a puzzled voice. "But if she comes to us there, we'll have deep water at our backs. How will we escape then?"

"The old tales say the water has healing powers," Tom said. "Perhaps it will be enough to save the people of Errinel."

Elenna looked curiously at him and leaned to whisper in his ear. "I thought you didn't believe in that story."

"I'm prepared to believe in anything right now," he murmured.

"But shouldn't we find the Beast

and defeat her straight away?"
Elenna asked.

"We will," Tom said firmly.
"But not before the villagers
have been taken to safety. We'll
spend the night at the lake – then
we'll find Soltra when the sun
comes up tomorrow. She'll be

more vulnerable then."

Word was quickly sent around the village that people should prepare provisions for the night. Then Tom led the villagers through the woods to the shining shores of the lake.

It looked beautiful in the golden light of the setting sun, hemmed with tall trees that were reflected in the wide, still waters. Looking out over its glowing expanse, Tom could almost believe that the lake really did have healing qualities. He certainly hoped so. But even if the lake had no special powers, at least the people were away from the village and perhaps harder for Soltra to track down.

It took a while for the large camp

to settle for the evening. The sun went down and the star-filled night turned the lake silver, but there was no sign of Soltra. Maybe the lake's waters were protecting them.

Small groups of villagers sat around fires, toasting bread and roasting jacket potatoes in the embers. Sometimes a few voices rose in song, but there was little laughter, and Tom could almost feel the subdued fear simmering.

Tom and Elenna sat at a fire with Uncle Henry and Aunt Maria. Silver was curled up close to the flames, enjoying the warmth. Storm stood quietly close by.

"So, Tom," Uncle Henry asked, "will you be staying here once you have defeated the Beast?"

Tom shook his head. "I have to find the rest of the Golden Armour," he said sadly, though he was happy that his uncle had such faith in him. He didn't add that the Dark Wizard had stolen the armour aand that each piece was guarded by a fearsome Beast. His aunt and uncle didn't need to know about that. They would only worry.

The fires died down and the villagers prepared for sleep. Soon, only Tom and Elenna and their animal friends were awake.

"I'll take first watch," Tom said to Elenna. "I'll wake you when I can't keep my eyes open any longer."

Elenna nodded. "Will Soltra

come?" she asked.

Tom stared into the trees, knowing the Beast was out there somewhere.

"I hope she does," he said. "Soltra attacked my home. While there is blood in my veins, I have to conquer her!"

6

THE GIFT

The lake's waters seemed to keep Soltra at bay. Tom woke ready to take on the Beast. The sun was bright over the treetops and the lakeside camp was bustling. He sprang up. But Aunt Maria stopped him with a gentle hand on his shoulder.

"Do you know what day it is, Tom?" she asked with a smile.

Tom shook his head, puzzled.

Elenna, Storm and Silver stood nearby. "You didn't tell me!" Elenna grinned.

He stared at her. "What are you talking about?"

"It's your birthday, Tom!" Uncle Henry said. "Did you forget?"

"Is it?" Tom gasped. So much had happened recently that he had lost count of the days.

"Yes, it is!" said Elenna. "Happy birthday!"

Silver barked and Storm neighed.

"If things were normal," Aunt Maria said, "we would celebrate properly, but..." Her voice trailed away.

"We have more urgent matters to

attend to," said Uncle Henry. "We'll celebrate when this is over. Now that it is daylight again, we should return to the village and call a meeting to discuss what we should do next."

"Yes, Uncle Henry, good idea," Tom said.

Elenna pulled him away from the others. "What's the point of that?" she whispered. "They won't be able to do anything to stop Soltra."

"I know," Tom replied softly. "But a village meeting will be the perfect cover for what I have to do. It will keep Uncle Henry and Aunt Maria busy and allow me to slip away unnoticed."

"You mean it will allow *us* to slip

away unnoticed," she corrected him.

Tom smiled. He was glad that he had such a brave and loyal friend as Elenna. "We can't let another night come without confronting the Beast," he told her. "Remember, when she enchanted Farmer Gretlin, she had her back to the setting sun. I think that maybe she can't stand to have her face towards sunlight. That might be our best weapon. If we can find her and force her into daylight, we might be able to defeat her."

"Farmer Gretlin was in his field near the marsh when he was turned to stone," Elenna said. "So we'll have to go there."

"Yes," Tom replied. "And there's no

time to waste. While there's blood in my veins, I'll save my village and defeat Soltra!"

At mid-morning the villagers gathered for their meeting in the main square. Tom and Elenna and the two animals stood out of sight behind the forge, getting ready to leave for the marsh.

Tom was pulling on his chainmail when his uncle appeared around the corner.

"You intend to leave the village while we talk," he said. "To find the Beast and fight her."

Tom nodded. There was no point trying to lie.

"I understand," Uncle Henry said gently. "But before you go, there is something I want to give you."

"What is it?" Tom asked. He felt proud, wearing the golden chainmail in front of his uncle. It glinted in the morning sunshine and Tom felt his heart grow stronger and stronger.

"It's in the forge," his uncle said. "Your father left it for you."

Tom's eyes widened in amazement – Uncle Henry had never mentioned a gift from his father before. His mind raced as he and Elenna followed his uncle into the forge. What could it be?

"Help me to move the anvil," said Uncle Henry.

Tom grasped one end of the anvil and helped to shift it across the floor. Then his uncle took a spade and began to dig into the hard-packed earth.

Shortly, the spade rang on something hard. A few moments later a square wooden box was

revealed, about a hand-span in length and depth.

Uncle Henry laid the box on the anvil and undid the metal clasp of the lid.

"It's yours to open," he told Tom.

Tom picked it up, his mind in a whirl as he wondered what secrets his father's gift might contain.

7

DESTINY AND DANGER

Eagerly, Tom opened the lid. Inside the box, something lay wrapped in a dark red velvet cloth. He lifted it out. It was heavy and solid. Tom unfolded the velvet wrap and gave a gasp of delight. It was a compass, made of gold and decorated with curling patterns.

"It's beautiful," said Elenna. "But

I've never seen a compass with such markings."

Engraved on the top of the compass were two words, one at either side of the needle.

"*Destiny*," Tom read quietly. "And *Danger*." He looked up at his uncle. "What does it mean?"

"Turn it over," Uncle Henry said. On the bottom were engraved the words: *For my son*.

Tom bit his lip, fighting back tears of joy, as well as regret that he had never known his father. He felt Elenna's calming hand on his shoulder.

"Taladon left this in my keeping when he departed Errinel on his own Quest," said Uncle Henry. "He asked that I give it to you on your first birthday as a hero." His eyes glowed with pride. "That day has come."

Tom looked at his uncle. He could feel his eyes brimming. "Did he leave any message for me?" he asked.

"No," his uncle replied. "But the compass needs no explanation. The needle will show you when to step forward to meet your destiny, and when to flee impossible danger. Your father believed that it would save your life one day."

"Perhaps today,"Tom murmured, gazing at the compass. "Thank you." He held the compass tightly; he had never felt so close to his lost father.

Then he gazed out of the doorway of the forge. It was time to go in search of Soltra the Stone Charmer.

Tom, Elenna, Silver and Storm stood at the edge of the marsh, gazing out over the barren wasteland. Even in the full light of the sun, coils and wreaths of fog drifted and crept low, like evil phantoms seeking their prey.

"Have you ever been here before?" Elenna asked.

Tom shook his head. "It's too treacherous," he said. "Aunt Maria always told me that only a fool would risk it."

"Or someone very brave," Elenna said.

Tom drew his sword and checked that his shield was securely fastened to his back. He could feel the weight of the compass in his pocket, tucked away under his chainmail. He felt strong in his heart, ready for the battle ahead. He had placed the golden helmet safely in Storm's saddlebag.

"How are we going to avoid Soltra's eye?" Elenna asked. Tom could tell from her voice that she was afraid.

"I'll find a way," Tom said.

"*We'll* find a way, you mean."

"No," Tom said firmly. "This time I have to do it alone. I want you to stay here with Storm and Silver."

Elenna's eyes were determined. "Never!" she said.

Tom shook his head with a rueful smile. Elenna was as strong-minded as he was. "Come on, then," he said. "But watch your footing. The further we go, the more dangerous the ground will become."

They moved slowly into the tall whispering reeds, Tom leading Storm, Silver keeping close to Elenna. The fog rose to cover them like a damp blanket. Soon, they came to stretches of black water and they had to pick their way along narrow paths of solid ground.

Storm became jittery, his hooves sinking into the soft earth. At last, he

neighed and pulled back, bringing
Tom to a halt. Tom patted his neck
and spoke softly to him, but it was
clear the brave stallion would go no
further. Silver crouched low, his ears
back and his eyes narrow slits.

"Will you stay back with Storm
and Silver?" Tom asked Elenna.
"We can't ask them to go any
further, and I don't want to leave

them here unprotected."

Elenna nodded, and slotted an arrow to her bow in readiness.

Tom stepped into the fog.

"Remember," he heard her call, "if you're in danger, summon one of the Good Beasts of Avantia."

Tom turned to wave, but already his companions had been swallowed by the fog. He was alone. His hand strayed to the compass tucked under his chainmail and the feel of it gave him comfort.

He squelched onwards, his feet sinking into the boggy ground as the pools of stagnant and stinking water began to widen. The fog was so thick now that he could not see the sun above his head. The reeds hissed and quivered.

He paused, breathing in the foul air, staring around. How would he find the Beast in this? She could be close enough to reach out and touch him, and he would hardly know it.

He wished he had brought the golden helmet to help him see. Perhaps the compass could assist, but before he had the chance to take it out a gentle voice spoke through the fog.

"Welcome to my home," it said.

Tom gripped his sword tightly. "Where are you?" he shouted.

"I am close," said the lovely voice. "Why do you not come and see me?"

Tom had never heard a voice so beautiful before.

He stepped forward, sheathing his sword. "Please?" he whispered, his senses drifting away from him. "Let me see you."

"Come," said the voice. "It is not far."

Tom stumbled on. But suddenly he tripped, losing balance, and staggered sideways, falling into the tall reeds. His foot plunged into deep slime, and he couldn't pull it out.

With a cry of fear, he found himself

knee-deep in thick, oozing mud. He struggled to free himself, but with every movement he sank deeper.

He was trapped!

8

THE MARSH

The oozing mud sucked at Tom's legs, dragging him slowly deeper, and suddenly he felt as if he had awoken from a dream. Thrashing about would do no good, he realised.

"I mustn't panic," Tom gasped. "I have to keep calm and find a way to pull myself out." He leaned forward and grasped at a tussock of long reeds, but they were slimy and he couldn't get a good grip.

He sank to his waist. How could he have been stupid enough to listen to that voice? Harsh, grating laughter filled his ears. *Malvel!* The evil wizard was mocking him, enjoying his triumph.

He heard Elenna distantly shouting, "Tom? Are you all right?"

Then there was another voice. "Come to me," sang Soltra's beautiful voice from across the marsh. "Come and stay with me for ever."

Tom tried to block out the Beast's voice, focusing all his concentration on pulling himself free. But it was hopeless. He gave a howl of anger and despair as the mud rose to his armpits. After all his battles against the Beasts of Avantia, was he going to die in a stinking mud-pit?

Then he saw something long and slender come hissing towards him through the fog. It curved downwards and hit the mud a few feet away from him. It was

an arrow – and tied to the shaft
was a rope.

"Elenna!" he gasped. He fought
with all his strength to reach the
arrow, leaning far over, his fingers
stretching out.

Elenna's faint voice called to him.
"Tom? Have you got it?"

"Almost!" he shouted. Finally,
his fingers closed around the rope.
"Yes!"

"Storm will pull you out!" yelled
Elenna.

Tom wrapped a loop of rope
around his wrist as it tightened.
For a few dreadful moments, the
mud clung to him. But then, slowly,
Tom felt himself being dragged out
of the slime and soon there was

firm earth under his fingers. He scrabbled and kicked with his legs and suddenly he was lying gasping on solid ground. He'd never been so close to death before.

He got to his feet, his legs shaking. "How did you know what to do?" he shouted to Elenna.

"I heard you cry out," she called back. "I shot the arrow towards the sound of your voice. I'm coming!"

"No!" Tom shouted. "Stay back – it's too dangerous." But he knew he needed help. Then he remembered the Good Beasts of Avantia, and one in particular: Arcta the Mountain Giant! With his sure footing and ability to destroy mountain mists, he could help

Tom through the marsh. Quickly Tom took his shield from his back and rubbed the magical token that Arcta had given him – an eagle's feather – desperately hoping that it would work.

Almost instantly he saw a shape coming towards him through the fog. Was it Soltra? Tom raised his mud-smeared shield and gripped the hilt of his sword tightly, ready to draw it once more.

The approaching shape was huge. Soon, it was close enough for Tom to be able to make out its features – the shaggy hair, the shambling gait and the familiar face peering down at him with its one friendly brown eye.

"Arcta!" Tom gasped with relief.
The giant swung his huge arms,
magically whisking away the fog
around them. Only then did Tom
see a second form standing dark
and still in a long robe among the
reeds.

"Welcome, Tom," sang the beautiful voice. "Come to me."

Long arms reached out, the robe rippling like black water. Tom stared at her, struggling to keep hold of his senses. But the voice was so lovely, and he could see that Soltra was tall and slender, the oval where her face should have been as smooth as glass and as white as milk.

Tom took a step towards her. Arcta let out a roar of warning.

"No, Arcta," Tom whispered, his mind suddenly as white and blank as the fog. "It's all right." He only wanted to be near her.

He stumbled towards Soltra, the fog closing behind him once

again. Her great eye opened.
Tom stopped. Then he took another
step forwards, gazing into the
beautiful eye.

9

THE GREAT EYE

A terrified voice shouted from deep within Tom's mind, *Look at the compass!*

Forcing his body to obey him, he drew the compass out of his pocket, holding it up in front of his eyes. The needle on the compass pointed to *Danger*.

"Oh!" he gasped, as the power of Soltra's gaze was broken. His mind clear again, he continued to walk slowly forwards, his eyes fixed on the compass. He had to get closer to the Beast if he was to defeat her.

"Come to me," crooned the voice.

"I'm coming," whispered Tom, his hand tightening on his shield. He was no longer hypnotised by the voice, but the Beast was now only a few strides away. The urge to look into her eye was growing again and he had to fight with all his strength to conquer it. His feet faltered and he stood still, breathing hard.

Soltra glided towards him. Then she reached into her robe and drew out a long grey whip. She swung her arm and the whip came snaking forward with a hiss.

Tom fended the whip off with his shield as Soltra swooped towards him then disappeared, swallowed by the fog, leaving him staggering.

With a peal of laughter, she reappeared behind him. The whip

cracked, raking along his back, sending him tumbling as she vanished out of sight.

How could he fight the Beast when he couldn't look at her?

Soltra lashed out again, the whip stinging as it bit into the flesh of his sword-hand. Tom turned, crying out with the pain, lunging into the empty fog.

The whip snapped once more, this time catching him around the legs and pulling him to his knees. Then a roar sounded. It was Arcta! He loomed over Tom, blowing the fog away with the power of his hands and his breath, allowing Tom to see.

Now Tom could make out the blurry white disk of the sun. Hope

rose in him. He stood up and turned to face the stone charmer. But as he did so, he foolishly allowed his gaze to rest upon the huge eye.

A feeling of peace and joy flooded him once again. He smiled, forgetting everything as an icy numbness seeped through his limbs.

"The cold is no danger," crooned Soltra's voice. "Stone is your destiny."

Arcta roared angrily and Malvel's scornful laughter filled Tom's head.

This time it was the mocking laughter that broke the spell. It filled Tom with determination, and the golden chainmail gave him renewed strength of heart. He tore his eyes from Soltra's face and the ice left his limbs.

"While there is blood in my veins," he shouted, "I will resist you!"

Arcta gave another roar, once more waving away the fog above Tom's head. Somehow the giant seemed to understand that Tom needed the sunlight to defeat Soltra. Golden light filtered down and Soltra was revealed again, but the afternoon sun was behind her now.

"Too late," Soltra sang as she moved forward. "The sun is low, the day is done. Come – be stone with me."

Tom gritted his teeth. If only

she could be made to stare into the sun!

Then he had an idea! Hastily Tom put the compass into his pocket and drew his sword. Lifting it above his head, he angled the blade to catch the sunlight on the steel edge. He had to be quick. Soon, he would be within reach of Soltra's coiling whip.

Just when he was beginning to lose hope, his blade caught the sun and a burst of golden light was reflected straight into Soltra's eye. She screamed in agony, lunging forward, her long arms reaching for him. As she did so, her robe swung open. Tom gasped in horror.

The Beast's body was a hideous skeleton – the thin white bones scraping together as she moved.

Then Tom caught his breath. The golden breastplate was clasped around Soltra's ribcage. Distracted by the sight of the shining piece of armour, he moved his sword arm and the sunlight shifted from her face.

Soltra let out a howl and her long fingers closed around Tom's throat, choking him in her frozen grip.

THE TOUCH OF DEATH

Tom could feel the strength fading from his muscles as he fought for breath, but he could do nothing as Soltra's deadly fingers squeezed the life out of him.

He was about to lose consciousness when he heard another roar. Arcta! The mountain giant appeared above him and

swung his great arm, striking
Soltra so that her grip loosened on
Tom's throat.

Tom didn't waste a moment. With
a final effort, he raised his sword.
He managed to catch the sunlight
on his blade once more, and the
great eye was flooded with the
brilliant reflection of the sun.

Soltra let out a terrible scream.
Her robe exploded and her skeleton
body crumbled into dust, the
golden breastplate clanging as it
hit the ground.

Panting, Tom stooped and
picked it up. The breastplate was
decorated with etched muscles, and
leather thongs and metal buckles
secured the sides. He clasped it

around himself, threading the thongs through the buckles. It fitted perfectly! He flexed his arms, feeling the muscles swell, and understood immediately that the breastplate gave him great

physical strength.

He looked up at Arcta. "Thank you!" he called. "I would have failed without your help!"

Arcta gave a roar of delight before turning and loping away, his huge body quickly lost in the fog. Tom knew that his deep bond with all the Good Beasts of Avantia would never be broken.

Tom turned and ran back through the fog towards where he hoped Elenna, Silver and Storm would be waiting for him. He longed to be with his friends again.

"Tom?" It was Elenna's voice! "I heard roaring and screaming. Are you all right?"

The shape of his friend, together

with Storm and Silver, appeared through the fog.

"Soltra is no more," Tom told them. "And look what she was wearing under her robe!"

"The next piece of the armour!" Elenna cried in delight. "That's the best birthday present ever! But what was the roaring we could hear? It reminded me of Arcta."

"I'll tell you everything on our way back to Errinel," Tom said with a smile.

The villagers greeted Tom and his companions with cheers of joy.

"We were hopeful that you had beaten the Beast when our

stone friends and Farmer Gretlin's oxen were returned to life," Uncle Henry said.

The three villagers who had been turned to stone waved at Tom, smiling cheerily.

"It was a close thing," Tom admitted. "My father's compass helped."

"Will you all stay for a while?" asked Aunt Maria. "We have a lot to celebrate!"

"I'm sorry, but we can't," Tom said, giving her a quick hug. "A friend of mine is missing, and I still have work to do for the king."

His uncle stepped forward. "Then go with our blessing," he said. "But return to us as soon as you can."

It was hard to leave Errinel so quickly, but Tom and Elenna and the two animals were soon on the road away from the village. They would be able to travel a long way before making camp for the night.

"Have you looked at the map?" Elenna asked. "Do we know where we're heading?"

"Not yet," Tom admitted. "I just needed to get out of the village quickly, or I wouldn't have wanted to leave at all." He looked back over his shoulder. "Sometimes battling the Beasts is not the hardest part of the Quest," he said.

"I understand," Elenna replied.

Suddenly, there was a clap of thunder and forked lightning struck the path ahead of them. Silver whined and Storm neighed in fear.

Malvel! He stood in their way, his arms stretched out so that his cloak was spread wide.

"We're not afraid of you!" Tom shouted, drawing his sword and brandishing it in the air, although

he knew he was looking at a vision.

The Dark Wizard smiled and drew one side of his cloak back. "Are you sure?" he asked as a shivering figure was revealed, kneeling on the path.

"Aduro!" Elenna gasped.

It was the Good Wizard. His blue cloak was missing and he looked pale.

"See how I have humbled the great Aduro," Malvel crowed. "How long do you think a boy like you can stand against me?"

"Long enough!" Tom shouted. "I'll rescue Aduro!"

"Listen well," snarled Malvel. "You may have won your golden breastplate, but the battle is not over yet!" The Dark Wizard's eyes

flashed. "If you continue your
Quest, there will be a heavy price
to pay."

Tom glared at him. "What will the
price be?" he asked.

"You shall see!" said Malvel.
There was another crack of thunder
and flash of lighting, then both
wizards were gone.

"What do you think he meant?"
Elenna asked, her voice subdued.

Tom looked at her. "I don't know,"
he said. "But it doesn't matter."
He flicked the reins and Storm
broke into a trot. "Nothing is
going to stop us from fulfilling the
Quest. Aduro sent us, and we must
complete it in order to rescue him."

Storm broke into a canter and

they raced along the road, Silver the wolf loping alongside them as they all headed into a new adventure.

Whatever lay ahead, Tom would defeat it. He had to. This was his destiny.

CONGRATULATIONS, YOU HAVE COMPLETED THIS QUEST!

At the end of each chapter you were awarded a special gold coin.
The QUEST in this book was worth an amazing 11 coins.

Look at the Beast Quest totem picture inside the back cover of this book to see how far you've come in your journey to become

MASTER OF THE BEASTS.

The more books you read, the more coins you will collect!

Do you want your own
Beast Quest Totem?
1. Cut out and collect the coin below
2. Go to the Beast Quest website
3. Download and print out your totem
4. Add your coin to the totem
www.beastquest.co.uk/totem

Don't miss the next exciting Beast Quest book, VIPERO, THE SNAKE MAN!

Read on for a sneak peek...

CHAPTER ONE

FAREWELL TO ERRINEL

Tom drew Storm to a halt a few miles beyond the village of Errinel. Turning in the saddle, he looked back.

"I wish we didn't have to leave,"

he said to his friend Elenna, who sat behind him on the magnificent stallion. "It's the first time I've been able to visit my home since I set out on the Beast Quest."

"It's hard," Elenna sympathised.

"I don't know when I'll see my uncle and aunt again," Tom said. He knew that until Avantia was safe from the Dark Wizard, Malvel, his Quest must come first – even before his family. It was his destiny to defeat six Evil Beasts and collect every piece of the magical Golden Armour, which Malvel had stolen and scattered across the kingdom. He already had three pieces: the helmet, which gave him extra-keen sight, the chainmail, which

bestowed strength of heart, and
the breastplate, which made him
physically strong. They were tucked
safely in Storm's saddlebag.

It's a good thing they're magical,
he thought now. *They hardly weigh
anything at all!*

Fear churned in his stomach as he
remembered how, after the defeat
of Soltra the Stone Charmer, Malvel
had appeared in a vision, warning
him there would be a heavy price
to pay if he completed this next
stage of the Quest. Even so, he was
determined to carry on. Malvel had
kidnapped their friend and protector,
Wizard Aduro, and only by finishing
the Quest could Tom and Elenna
hope to set him free. Aduro himself

had told them so.

"Tom." Elenna shook his shoulder gently. "We have to go. Another Evil Beast is waiting for us."

"I know." Energy flooded through Tom as he pledged himself once more to his Quest. He leant forward to pat Storm on the neck. "Let's go, boy."

Read
VIPERO THE SNAKE MAN
to find out more!

FIGHT THE BEASTS,
FEAR THE MAGIC

Are you a BEAST QUEST mega fan?
Do you want to know about all the latest news,
competitions and books before anyone else?

Then join our Quest Club!

Visit the BEAST QUEST website
and sign up today!

www.beastquest.co.uk

Discover the new Beast Quest mobile game from

Available free on iOS and Android

  amazon.com

Guide Tom on his Quest to free the Good Beasts
of Avantia from Malvel's evil spells.

Battle the Beasts, defeat the minions,
unearth the secrets and collect
rewards as you journey through the
Kingdom of Avantia.

DOWNLOAD THE APP TO BEGIN
THE ADVENTURE NOW!